Lord Lindum's Anus Mirabilis

By a Gentleman

[I have just received an anonymous and rather pompous tweet claiming that *Anus Mirabilis* should be *Annus Mirabilis* because *annus* means 'year' in Latin and *anus* means 'bumhole'. I shall ignore it because it is obviously a prank. You know what Twitter is like. I include this note in the interests of scholarship. - Ed.]

Quirinal Press

LN2 5RT

Copyright © Ian Thomson 2021

Ian Thomson has asserted his right under the Copyright, Designs and Patents Act 1988 to be identified as the author of this work

This book is a work of fiction. The characters within it are not intended to represent any persons, living or dead. Any apparent resemblance is purely co- incidental.

Lindum Towers

Christmas 2020

C hristmas Eve, 2020

'Look here, I know it's only teatime but given that it's a tad parky out there, Fiskerton, do you think it might be above board for a chap to have a snifter of something seasonal? Eh?'

'Certainly, sir. There can be no reasonable objection, I believe. Might I suggest a glass of ginger wine?'

'Capital, capital! The very thing. After all, it's hardly alcoholic at all. Just pop, really. A child might quaff a pint of it and be none the worse for wear.'

'Well, sir, that is not entirely the case. I would venture to suggest that the child might be very poorly indeed.'

'Fiddlesticks! I don't pay you to venture things. Bring me a glass forthwith. Wait, may as well bring me the bottle.'

'Very well, sir.'

'And half a dozen mince pies.'

'As your lordship wishes.'

'With brandy cream.'

'I fear that given the gout attack that laid your lordship prostrate yesterday I am constrained to ask: Is that wise?'

'Probably not but I don't give a badger's nadgers. Now get on with it. Can't you see that I am wasting away from hunger and thirst while you fanny around?'

'My most abject apologies, my lord.'

'You can cut the bowing and scraping too, you fool. Now scuttle off and get my refreshments *toot sweet*. Oh, and Fiskers, none of your parsimonious *smearings* of cream. I want bloody great galloping masculine dollops of it.

Later

'Where the devil have you been, Fiskerton? I've been ringing for at least twenty seconds.'

'I have been somewhat preoccupied, your lordship. I have made potato salad for the Boxing Day buffet. I have prepared the carrots and sprouts for tomorrow. I have made bread sauce. I have cleaned the silver and vacuumed the whole house. I have decorated the tree in the great hall with baubles, each of which has been lovingly handmade. I was wrapping your gift when you rang. I am sorry to have been so tardy.'

'Good heavens, man, you have quite exhausted me with your recital of good deeds. Bring me a sherry at the double.'

'Very good, sir.'

'Then you may take a short break.'

'Thank you, sir. I would welcome the opportunity to pop upstairs and give Nanny Branston a small gift.'

'Good Lord, man, upstairs? I said take a break, not a holiday.'

Later

'Do you know what strikes my festive fancy at this precise hour and minute, Fiskerton? Along with a nightcap, as it were.'

'No, sir, I can't say I do.'

'I believe a fat slab of Mrs Washingborough's chocolate cake might be good for the old constitution. What?'

'Well, to be perfectly candid…'

'Yes?'

'I imagine it might, sir.'

'Attend to it, will you?'

'At once, sir.'

'Oh, and you may have a couple of water biscuits with beef dripping.'

'Your lordship's generosity is legendary in these parts, sir.'

'Well, it's nearly Christmas, you know.'

Christmas Day

'Put the box of corn plasters away, Fiskerton. Yes, I know it's not every day that a butler receives such a generous gift from his master, but I venture to think you have much to do today. Now run my bath for me, would you, there's a good chap. And then I think I should like something fizzy to drink while you get on with the sprouts.

'PUT THE PLASTERS AWAY, MAN! And cheer up, for God's sake. You've got a face on you like a smacked arse!'

Later
The Servant's Hall
Lindum Towers

'Ah, Mr Fiskerton, I see his lordship made you a present of corn plasters too.'

'Quite so, Mrs Washingborough.'

'I cannot think why he thought I should have need of them. I am not troubled by corns, bunions, ingrowing toe-nails, athlete's foot, flat feet nor any other problem with my trotters, though my knees have been playing up something shocking. Doctor said two years ago (before he done a run-ner, that is) that we would need to think of knee replace-ments soon. What with, I don't know. Wheels would be a good idea, I reckon. What possessed his lordship to give us both corn plasters I can't imagine.'

'I understand that Scampton received the same gift. I fancy that, since he is employed by his lordship as chauffeur, gardener, gamekeeper, estates manager, woodsman, groom and carpenter, he might not unreasonably be said to be "run off his feet".'

'Very droll, Mr F.'

'I was not intending to be "droll", Mrs Washingborough. And pray refrain from addressing me as Mr F. It is quite indecorous. Let us be charitable and assume that his lordship is forearming us in case of some future infirmity.'

'Charitable, my eye. Corn plasters indeed. And what did you give his lordship?'

'I am uncertain what business it is of yours, Mrs Washingborough, but if you must know, I gave his lordship a copy of *Bleak House* by Charles Dickens.'

'*Bleak House? Bleak House?* This is Bleak House, if you want to know the truth. With respect, Mr Fiskerton, you're off your chump. You bought him a beautiful edition of *A Christmas Carol* last year and what happened to it? I found it in a charity shop when they opened up last July. I knew it was the one because you'd signed it. Well. It was in pristine condition, never been touched, let alone read. The same will happen to your *Bleak House*, you mark my words. And what do you get for your generosity? Corn plasters.'

'Mrs Washingborough, I have had occasion to speak to you before on your want of loyalty. It behoves those of us in service to be respectful to our employers under all circumstances.'

'Respectful? Stuff and nonsense! He don't deserve no respect. Old Scrooge that he is. Corn plasters? Lord save us, what did that cost him? Next to nothing. And he ain't even got the imagination to get us all something different. We've all got the same thing. Corn plasters.'

'Now that is not entirely true, Mrs Washingborough. Scopwick received a bar of soap.'

'For the stench?'

'For the stench, as you say. That was clearly his lordship's intention. There never was a boy in the history of the realm who stank so remarkably as his lordship's boot boy.'

'He won't use it.'

'Indeed he won't, Mrs Washingborough, the wretched child had eaten half of it before I took it from him.'

'There goes his Lordship's bell, Mr Fiskerton.'

'I wonder he is still alive considering what he consumed at dinner: Oysters, Clear Soup, Dover Sole, Goose with all the trimmings, Stilton cheese with grapes, your exquisite plum pudding with white sauce, coffee and petit-fours. And a different wine with each course to boot. I would be astonished if he could even move.'

'Except to ring the bell.'

'Quite so. I'd better see what he wants before he flies into one of his apoplexies.'

The Drawing Room

'Ah, there you are at last, you unutterable sloth. Bring me an axe.'

'Whatever for, your lordship?'

'Don't argue with me, man. Bring me an axe. I am going to destroy the television. I am going to reduce it to matchwood. I am going to to turn it into toothpicks. Don't stand there gawping, man. Bring me the chopper.'

'I fear the set might explode, my lord.'

'All the better.'

'Might I enquire what has brought on this fit of rage against the box?'

'You might have thought that on Christmas Day, of all days, there might be something worth watching. But no, nothing but this milk and water diet, this plebeian pabulum, this insipid populist pap. What the devil do I want with *Call the Midwife*, *Strictly Come Dancing* and *Gogglebox*? Whatever happened to *Morecambe and Wise*? Eh? Get out of that. You can't, can you? As for *Mrs Brown's Boys*…bring me the axe.'

'There must be something…'

'There is NOTHING, I tell you! It all started careering downhill when Dr Who became a woman. Insane. This is what comes of giving women the vote, you know. I should have put a stop to it at the time. I should have gone down to London and denounced the bill in the Lords. I would have changed history.'

'I think that unlikely, sir.'

'Do you doubt my oratorical powers, Fiskerton?'

'Not in the least, your lordship. However, when the *Representation of the People Act, 1928*, accorded women over 21 the vote on the same terms as men, your lordship was not yet born.'

'A detail.'

'Of course, my lord.'

'And then there's the plot. They have such fancy plots on *Doctor Who* these days. Couldn't tell what was going on.'

'To be fair, your lordship did consume a considerable quantity of Burgundy...'

'Are you suggesting that I am drunk, you sewer? By God, you'll go the same way as the idiot box. Smashed to bits. Drunk? *Moi?*'

'Far be it from me...'

'I may be a trifle squiffy, perhaps, but I would defy anybody sober to work out what was going on. I would defy a teetotal nun. You knew where you were with Daleks and Cidermen.'

'Cybermen.'

'That's what I said: Cidermen. They were sideboards.'

'Cyborgs.'

'Exactly. Anyway, I don't pay my television licence for this heap of buffalo dung.'

'Begging your lordship's pardon but you haven't paid your television licence since 2011. You put off the detector van people with good claret and a bribe which exceeded the arrears. They returned the following year, and you chased them away with a twelve bore. Eventually, you had Scampton encircle the estate with barbed wire, and you had the drive mined. They have not returned. The demands keep arriving, of course, but they are filed with other tradesmen's bills.'

'In the Aga, yes. Quite right. Stop trying to distract me. Get the axe, damn your eyes!'

'If I might make a less dramatic suggestion for your lordship's entertainment?'

'This had better be good.'

'I took the liberty, whilst shopping for your lordship's Christmas festivities, of acquiring a number of Teletubbies box sets. There are 53 episodes in total. Now, if I were to bring your lordship some fine Armagnac and some Belgian liqueur chocolates, and settle you down to watch 'Here Come the Teletubbies', might that go some way towards cooling your lordship's temper?'

'You know, Fiskers, you old buttock, from time to time, you have some corking light bulb moments. Just once in a while I could almost swear you were human.'

30 December, 2020

'Oh, my lord, my lord. Oh, happy day!'

'Good heavens, Fiskerton, whatever is the matter? Compose yourself. You're up and down like a bride's nightie.'

'My lord, AstraZenica has been approved!'

'Who has? Zena the Warrior Princess? Can't say I approve really. Bit of a tart that one, if you ask me. Huge norks, mind you.'

'No, no, no, my lord. The Oxford/AstraZenica vaccine has been approved. One day, this dreadful plague can be put behind us. Sooner perhaps, rather than later.'

'Good show. Oxford, eh? British then? Spanking good show.'

'Indeed, your lordship. The elderly and clinically vulnerable will be eligible first.'

'That means me and you, then Fiskerton, doesn't it? Well me anyway.'

'It does.'

'Well get my coat, man. We'll go and get jabbed forthwith.'

'I'm afraid we shall have to wait until we are summoned but, rest assured, we will be in the first cohort because of our advanced years.'

'Quite right. And it will be administered by Zena the Warrior Princess, you say. Wizard! Like to take a closer look at those norks.'

'No, your lordship has not got the situation wholly right. Shall I begin at the beginning?'

'Well, that was an arse of a year, wouldn't you say, Fiskers, old boot?'

'It was calamitous, your lordship.'

'Imprisoned in one's own bolt hole for months on end, separated from one's chums, excursions to the jolly old Pole-cat forbidden, wearing masks like bandits, worrying about whether you'll be able to wipe your bum decently, shortages of hand appetiser…'

'Sanitiser.'

'Shortages of hand appetiser. *Emmerdale* running short of material. No theatre, music, nightclubs. Do you think things will ever get better, ancient retainer?'

'We must hope so, your lordship.'

'Hope springs eternal in the human beast, eh?'

'Breast.'

'What?'

'Hope springs eternal in the human *breast*.'

'Breast? Breast? What on earth has got into you, Fiskerton? Have you developed Tourette's or something?'

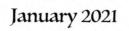

January 2021

January 1st

'I say, Fiskerton. What's the weather forecast for tomorrow?'

'There may be up to two centimetres of snow in Lincoln, sir.'

'Two centimetres? What's that in real money?'

'Just over three quarters of an inch, sir.'

'Not like the snows of our youth, then? Eh? What?'

'Indeed not, sir, I remember it took me most of the morning to clear your Lordship's drive in 1970.'

'And are you prepared for tomorrow?'

'Indeed I am, sir. It will be but a mere dusting. I venture to think a tablespoon might suffice to clear the way should your Lordship wish to sally out.'

'We shall see. I think a glass of port might help me to contemplate that eventuality with fortitude. Just leave the decanter within reach, there's a good chap. Then I think you should put two hot water bottles in my bed tonight, don't you?'

'You are a good woman, Mrs Washingborough. I am most grateful for your ministrations.'

'Now don't you mention it, Mr Fiskerton. Least I can do after what his lordship put you through. Just you keep your feet in that mustard bath and your head over that steaming bowl of Vick. Keep the towel over your head and breathe deep. I could rub some Vick on your chest if you like.'

'Thank you kindly but I don't think that will be necessary and I believe I can dispense with the towel now. I can breathe without shuddering and the sense has returned to my nose.'

'The forecast was wrong then?'

'The forecast was indeed wrong. In this part of the county at least four inches of snow fell overnight. I believe that in the city it was much less.'

'But what exactly was going on out there. I stood on a stool in the pantry, but you know how high the window is. I could only see people's feet.'

'It is a sorry tale, Mrs Washingborough, a sorry tale, but I will not spare you the details. When I took his lordship his morning tea and opened the curtains of the master bedroom, the view was enchantment itself. A blanket of purest white stretched from the balustrades below, completely hiding the parterres, and reached down to the ha-ha. Beyond, the meadows were similarly overlain with the snowy coverlet. The great Lindum Oak, in which the Duke of Canwick is said to have hidden during the Civil War, dressed only in his wig and a pair of silk stockings, stood with its great boughs bending under the weight of snow upon them. The cattle stood bemused in the fields. The fountain before the house was frozen over and the statue of Cupid stood in the ice-bound midst with icicles hanging from his nose, his ears and his... thing.'

'Oh, Mr Fiskerton, you paint a magical picture.'

'His lordship thought so too when I moved him to the wing chair closer to the window. In fact, he was enraptured. Alas, however, the vista also gave him ideas.'

'Oh dear.'

'Precisely. Could you top up the hot water in this foot bath, do you suppose? I find it most comforting.'

'Of course. But do go on.'

'His lordship proposed a snowball fight with himself pitted against the staff. I smelled a rat immediately. "That would hardly be fair," I said, hoping to put him off. "After all, your wheelchair has very limited manoeuvrability and, in the snow, virtually none."

'"Ah, but I have a stratagem," he said. "You will marvel at the ingenuity of it. I shall need two large insulated cool bags such as we use on shooting parties, and a clothes peg."'

'A clothes peg?'

'A clothes peg, Mrs Washingborough. You see, his lordship's stratagem was to employ Scopwick to make snowballs for him and, the clothes peg was necessary…'

'Because of the stench.'

'Exactly so. The boy was employed in making snowballs which were stored in the cool bags before battle commenced. His lordship sat in his wheel chair by the arbour, well-wrapped in rugs and blankets, wearing a muffler, fur hat and gloves, with the clothes peg on his nose. When Scopwick had ensured that his magazine was full, he required Scampton and myself to stand within ten feet of him while he pelted us with snowballs.'

'Outrageous! I hope you pelted him back.'

'Indeed no. We were not permitted to respond. In fact, we were not permitted to evade the artillery by ducking - we were not permitted to move at all.'

'Damnable!'

'He kept up the tirade for nigh on two hours till all about the ground was quite denuded of snow, and Scopwick was hard pressed to keep up the supply of weapons. I believe the wretched boy was enjoying our discomfiture, and he will feel the weight of my hand when next I am upwind of him.

'By now, a rapid thaw had set in and the snowballs were turning into mush in his lordship's hands. Scampton was required to wheel him back to the house, and I was commanded to bring him coffee and brandy. I left him soundly asleep before the fire, and I believe we can hear him snoring, even below stairs.'

'And that is when I found you sitting on the stone steps to the kitchen, half-frozen to death.'

'I believe I might have perished but for your matronly attentions, Mrs Washingborough.'

'Think nothing of it, Mr Fiskerton. But what of poor Scampton?'

'The man is a hero. He withstood the battery with fortitude. I hope he is sitting before a blazing fire in the gatehouse with a tankard of mulled ale.'

'And Scopwick?'

'No doubt he is snuggled down in the piggery where his lordship insists he makes his bed...'

'Because of the stench.'

'Precisely. The sows will keep him warm, though I have a feeling that one of these days even they will find the boy's aroma too ripe.'

January 8th

'Now, let me get these new regulations right in my head, Fiskerton, you old toadstool. First, one is obliged to work from home. Well, that's not a problem for you, is it? It's what you do. And personages of my rank and class don't work.'

'Perish the thought.'

'Second, these bubbles. Now as I understand it, one can form a bubble with another household so long as is quite exclusive.'

'I believe so, my lord.'

'So that if I were to pay a visit to Lady Skellingthorpe at Hartsholme House, and she were to repay the visit at Lindum Towers, we would be in a bubble so long as we didn't frolic around elsewhere.'

'That is my understanding too, your lordship. Is your lordship planning to enter into a bubble with her ladyship, may I ask?'

'By the lord Harry, Fiskers! What lewd talk! You can be remarkably coarse sometimes, old fartleberry.'

'I believe your lordship may have set me up with that one.'

'Possibly. Just possibly.'

'Very jocular, my lord. Almost sidesplitting, one might say.'

January 16th

'Mrs Washingborough has just informed me that Her Majesty the Queen and His Royal Highness, the Duke of Edinburgh, have both been vaccinated.'

'How does she know?'

'She heard it on the wireless.'

'Who? The Queen? Her Majesty heard it on the wireless?'

'No, your lordship, Mrs Washingborough heard it on the wireless. Her Majesty has been vaccinated.'

'But that is wonderful. What a fine example to the nation. We must follow her lead and get jabbed at once, Fiskerton. Get my coat!'

'I think I have already explained that we must wait until we are called, your lordship.'

'By whom? Almighty God?'

'The NHS.'

'Ah.'

February

February 3rd

'I say, Fiskerton, you rabid mongrel, take a look at this in the *Torygraph*. Captain Sir Tom Moore has died at the age of 100. He's the gallant cove who walked a hundred lengths of his garden for NHS charities. Raised over 32 million ackers. I could do that, you know.'

'I fear your lordship means that you want me to wheel you up and down the garden a hundred times. I don't think that would quite do.'

'You're a miserable old dishcloth somtimes, Fiskerton, do you know that? Oh, very well, but something must be done to celebrate this extraordinary man. Go up on the roof immediately and fire a one hundred gun salute.'

'I am afraid that is not possible. Your lordship may recall that there is no ammunition left. Besides the cannon exploded on the occasion of the Queen's Silver Jubilee in 1977 and is no longer functional. The last two cannonballs upended a young stag in the deer park and completely destroyed the gazebo.'

'Happy days, eh, Fiskerton?'

'For some, my lord. For some.'

February 20th

'Lord Lindum! Lord Lindum!'

'What is it?, Fiskerton? What is the matter? Is it the End Times?'

'No, your Lordship. It is excellent news! A letter from the NHS. We can apply online for immunisation at the Lincolnshire Fairground any time from now on.'

'Oh bliss. But you must do it for me, Fiskerton. I have never quite got the hang of this Internest thing.'

'Internet, your lordship.'

'Yes, that. New-fangled affair. Can't quite grasp it.'

'Now you know that is not entirely true, my lord. You have had a number of Facebook posts removed for breaching their guidelines. You have been banned from Twitter on three occasions for lewd images and for saying a lady MP was as attractive as a caribou stork and that a very senior member of Her Majesty's Government was a a necrophiliac. You very nearly invested the entire estate in a Ponzi scheme until I stopped you.'

'You always were a spoilsport, Fiskerton.'

Later

'I have made the booking, my lord. We are expected on February 28th at 1300 hours.'

'And what time is that in real money?'

'One o'clock, sir.'

'Well, why didn't you rogering well say so, you polly-wog? Now what does this inoculation entail? Eh?'

'The vaccine is injected directly into the muscle of the upper arm.'

'Don't like the sound of that, Fiskers. I say, I don't like the sound of that. I shall ask for a general anaesthetic.'

'I very much doubt if that will be an available option, your lordship.'

'They'll do it for me, Fiskerton. You mark my words. No doubt about it. They'll do it for me.'

Later
The Kitchen

'No, no, no, Mr Fiskerton, I won't go, I tell you.'

'But you must, Mrs Washingborough. The vaccine will protect you.'

'From what? Nobody has left this house for months. Nobody comes, nobody goes. How could the virus possibly get in here? Deliveries are made to the gate house, and Scampton disinfects them before bringing them up to the big house. I'm more likely to get swine flu from Scopwick. I says no and I means no.'

'But there is no need to be afraid of a little prick.'

'I am not afraid of Scopwick and I'll charge you to watch your language in my kitchen.'

'I don't mean Scopwick, woman. I mean the needle.'

'I'm not afraid of no needle, Mr Fiskerton, and that's for certain. I have had more needles stuck in me, in my days, than Marie Antoinette's pincushion. I have been stuck like a hedgehog, I have. Like a porklypine. I have had injections for scarlet fever, mumps, measles, dippytheria, malaria, the black death, the red death, the palsy, the quotidian ague, the influenza, the outfluenza - you name it, I have been jabbed for it. Oh, I'm not afraid of no needle, Mr Fiskerton. It's 'im.'

''im?'

''im upstairs. His lordship.'

'Oh, *him*. Oh come now, Mrs Washingborough. It really is time you got over this phobia.'

'I have not been in the same room with that monster this ten years past, and I will be damned if I am going to get in a car with him now.'

'Don't you think that being stricken by the coronavirus is a more terrible prospect?'

'Nowhere near.'

February 28th

'Is your lordship quite ready? Scampton has brought the Bentley round. It is with great difficulty that I have prevailed upon Mrs Washingborough to sit in the front while I sit in the back with your lordship. That way she will not see you face to face.'

'Preposterous. Remind me why I employ that woman.'

'Her lemon drizzle cake, her banana bread, her cherry clafoutis, her apricot flan, her sticky toffee pudding, her brandy snaps…'

'Ah yes…'

Later
On the way to the Lincolnshire Showground

'Are we nearly there yet?'
'Not far now, your lordship.'
'I want to wee.'
'There will be facilities at the vaccination centre.'
'I want to wee now.'
'Here, have a Werther's Original toffee. It will take your mind off it.'

His lordship leans forward just behind Mrs Washingborough

'BOO!'

Mrs Washingborough screams

Later
The return journey

'I don't know what all the fuss is about. Didn't feel a thing. In fact, I didn't know he'd done it. "You'll just feel a slight scratch," he said. "Well get on with it then," I said. "It's all done," he said, 'Finished. You can roll up your sleeve." Friendly sort of cove.'

'Your lordship was very brave.'

'I was. Nobody could call me a cowardly nancy boy. It's a rum do, though, Fiskerton. I was expecting a lady nursie, you know, with norks, and I got a fellah. By the way, Fiskers, old bedpan, why do they say, "You'll feel a little scratch" rather than, "You'll feel a little prick"?'

'To avoid any ambiguity, I fancy. Especially if the nurse is a male.'

'What? Oh yes, I see. I say that's very droll, Fiskerton.'

'Thank you, your lordship.'

'If a little saucy. No, I have to say, I took my punishment like a true Briton. Unlike Washingborough. What a disgraceful performance!'

'I don't believe Mrs Washingborough was afraid of the injection. I believe her wailing and quivering were the result of the trauma she suffered in the car as a result of the shock you gave her.'

'Stuff and nonsense. Woman's a fool. Where is she now by the way.'

'She refused point blank to get into the car again. She is hitch hiking back to Lindum Towers. We may not see her for some time.'

March

March 6th

'I told you before: the END TIMES are upon us. Look at this in *The Daily Telegraph*. A great fiery meteor appears to have flashed through the night sky in Goucestershire before falling into somebody's garden near Stow-in-the-Wold. It is a judgement upon them. You mark my words!'

'For what misdemeanout exactly are these people being judged, your lordship?'

'Oh, something heinous, no doubt, some filthy iniquity unfit to be named. Abominations for which the people of Gloucestershire are notorious.'

'Such as?'

'I just said that they were unfit to be named, didn't I? Don't be obtuse, Fiskerton.'

'It's just that I understood the landing of the meteorite on these people's garden path to be quite a random, haphazard event.'

'No, I assure you. It is a sign of God's wrath upon the sins of Gloucestershire. Sins which could well be as transmissible as the coronavirus. I, say, Fiskers, old goose - is Gloucestershire far from here?'

'It is quite the other side of the country, my lord.'
'Good. Let's keep it that way.'

March 8th

'Who is this Oprah Winfrey woman anyway, Fiskerton?'

'She is an American talk show host, your lordship.'

'That is what I thought. Now, pray tell me what on earth a Prince of the realm is doing on an American talk show, for that is what this so-called interview is, is it not?'

'I couldn't possibly say, sir.'

'You wouldn't get Her Majesty the Queen on an American talk show, now would you? Stand up when I mention the Queen.'

'I am standing, your lordship.'

'Well, kneel then. I say, you wouldn't get her to demean herself by taking part in a circus like this, would you?

'Certainly not, your lordship.'

'Certainly not. O dear, O dear. Harry, my boy, your grandmother must be spinning on her throne if she is watching this codswallop.'

'I must say, it does appear most unseemly.'

'Turn it off. Turn it off. She's wittering on about the Little Mermaid falling in love with her prince. Hand me that vase. I think I'm going to throw up.'

March 27th

'The old *Telegraph* is full of meaty news today, Fiskers, old cauliflower. Listen to this: "A statutory instrument was introduced to criminalise travel from the realm". What is a statutory instrument? Is it like a trombone?'

'No, your lordship, it is a form of legislation. In this case it makes leaving the country a criminal offence.'

'Were we planning to leave the country?'

'No, sir. Your lordship doesn't like "abroad".'

'Oh, I've no objection to "abroad", Fiskerton, it's Johnny Foreigner I can't do with. Jabbering away and eating molluscs and amphibians and driving backwards. Mind you, they are responsible for some good things. Oh dear! Hell's teeth!'

'What is the matter, your lordship?'

'Panic stations!'

'Why, sir?'

'Does this mean that there will be no vino and fromidge?'

'I don't believe so, sir, and besides your cellar and pantry are well stocked.'

'Thanks be to God for that.'

'Indeed.'

'Now this is truly concerning: it says here that a fiery meteor has been seen by day in Dorset, Somerset and Devon and many people have reported a noise like a sonic boom.

The end is nigh, Fiskerton. We must prepare to meet our doom. Are these places near Lincolnshire?'

'No, my lord, they are in what is known as the West Country. Even further away than Gloucestershire.'

'That's something, I suppose. But no! Wait! Look at this: "A walrus has settled on the rocks in Pembrokeshire." It is the END TIMES, I tell you! Doom! Doom!'

April

April 8th

'Any interesting news on the wireless, Fiskerton. I had a little snooze and missed it.'

'Haircuts have been decriminalised in Scotland.'

'Absurd. Have the poor wee Scots been obliged to dance on swords and toss cabers, with the hair over their eyes like highland cattle?'

'It appears so, your lordship. Moreover, they are forbidden from crossing the border into England without lawful excuse.'

'Well, that's no hardship for us, old tattie. We don't want them hooting and skirling all over England's green and pleasant land, now do we? This will be the work of Minnie the Minx, I imagine.'

'I presume your lordship is referring to the First Minister of Scotland.'

'Thou sayest aright. I say, Fiskerton, what about this: ""The virgin sturgeon needs no urgin"", what?'

'Very diverting, sir.'

'There's a merkin lurkin' in the gherkin firkin.'

'I think it's time for your lordship's medication.'

His Lordship has been watching the Boat Race on the television. Clare Balding is summing up the action.

'And Cambridge has won the 166th Boat Race and the 75th women's race too, both rowed on the Great Ouse at Ely to deter crowds.'

'Hogwash, woman! Should be declared null and void. Light blues on their own patch, knew where every bulrush was, cutting into Oxford's water, brazen cheats, blind referee! Call that a river? It's a bloody canal. Call that an eight? Bunch of inbreds.'

'Might not your lordship, as an Oxford man, be just a tiny bit biased?'

'Well, of course, I'm biased, man! That's the whole point, isn't it? Mind you, its a very long time since I was up at the House.'

'I have often wondered which of your lordship's intellectual gifts was foremost in gaining your admission to that august university.'

'Oh, you can stop wondering, old knickerbocker. The old title was enough to get you in back then. Three glorious years of wine, women and song - and gambling. Didn't do a stroke of work and ended up with a Douglas.'

'A Douglas?'

'A third, man. A Douglas Hurd. It was known as a 'gentleman's third', and was probably worth more than a first in some quarters. Showed you had chutzpah, don't you know.'

'That explains a good deal, your lordship.'

'They wanted me to row stroke for the college eight, you know. I lasted one training session. You had to get up at sparrowfart, and row up and down in the freezing cold with some maniac on a bicycle pedalling alongside shouting abuse at you through a megaphone. Well, I wasn't having that. The old constitution wasn't up to having to get up before I'd even gone to bed. And besides, there was this story that was doing the rounds about a Cambridge College - I forget which - whose oarsmen had thrown their cox into the river. Poor little blighter was impaled on the handlebars of a bicycle lying on the riverbed. Well, that was a bit too bloody even for me. I didn't want to be associated with such people. Took up poker instead. Safer. Good money.'

April 9th

'Your lordship will be pleased to hear that there has been a dramatic fall in deaths and hospitalisations.'

'So I see from the paper. And Boris has had a haircut. It is an omen. Perhaps we are not in the END TIMES after all. Perhaps we might even begin to hope.'

'Indeed, after the ghastliness of 2020, perhaps this year might yet prove to be an *annus mirabilis*.'

'Is that Welsh?'

'Latin, you lordship. It means a 'year of wonders'.

'Yes, yes, I know that. Just went blank for a moment. I read classics at the Varsity, you know.

'Ah.'

'Not strictly true, of course. I didn't read anything most of the time.

Later

'Well, that's put the kibosh on your 'year of wonders', Fiskerton. The Duke of Edinburgh has popped his clogs. Bring me a black tie. This is a House of Mourning.'

April 17th
The Servants' Hall

'I fear things have taken a lugubrious turn, Mrs Washingborough, just as they were looking a little rosier. Delhi has gone into complete lockdown. India has been put on the red list. And the Indian variant is spreading like wildfire.'

'And then there was the poor Duke's funeral this afternoon, Mr Fiskerton.'

'I hardly think he was a poor Duke; I should think he was a very rich Duke indeed.'

'You knows what I mean, Mr Fiskerton. It was a fig-leaf of speech.'

'His lordship has taken it very hard. He recorded the funeral, and has watched it three times already. The sight of Her Majesty sitting alone in the quire had him howling. If you ask me, I find it rather out of proportion. The man was just short of a hundred, and one cannot live for ever.'

'What is that bizarre noise, Mr Fiskerton?'

'I am afraid his lordship is on the roof again. As you know, Scampton and I have the devil's own trouble getting him up there in his wheelchair. It is difficult to negotiate the time-worn steps when one is being constantly rapped on the head with a walking stick. Scopwick is up there with him - at a prescribed distance, of course.'

'Because of the stench?'

'Because of the stench. His lordship has bidden him toll the bell in the north tower at intervals of twenty seconds. The strangeness of what you hear is partly due to two things. Firstly, the boy cannot count that far. Secondly, he is attempting to play a tune on a single bell which accounts for the absurd syncopations.

'Meanwhile, his lordship scoured the library before being carried aloft, looking for books with 'death' in the title. He is reading from *Death in the Afternoon* by Mr Hemingway through a megaphone. Fortunately, the nearest habitation is miles away so he is declaiming in vain to the livestock and to the Lincolnshire wolds.'

'Why do you say fortunately, Mr Fiskerton?'

'Because, Mrs Washingborough, I believe the text he has chosen is not in the least appropriate to commemorate the demise of Her Majesty's royal consort.

'*Death in the Afternoon* is about bullfighting.'

April 30th

'Well, there we are. Second jab, all done and dusted. I expect we're both immortal now, are we?

'Well, hardly, your lordship.'

'Invulnerable then.'

'Not exactly.'

'Well what then?'

'Significantly protected, I'd say.'

'You would, would you? I'm a protected species, am I? Like bats, great crested newts, otters, water voles, and badgers?

'Dear God! The times we live in!'

May

May 1st

'O, the month of May, the merry month of May.
So frolic, so gay, and so green, so green,
O, and then to my true love, did I say,
Sweet Hippolyta, thou shalt be my summer's queen.'

'Your lordship is in fine spirits, this beautiful morning.'

'And in fine voice too, though I say it myself.'

'To a point, your lordship. To a point. And what, may I enquire, has brought on this unwonted merriment?'

'Because it is springtime, my old botty-burp. You cannot go about with that sarcophagus face. "In the spring a young man's fancy lightly turns to thoughts of love." That's Tennyson, that is. Alfred Lawn Tennyson was a Lincolnshire man, you know. Big fellow. Had an Irish wolfhound called Nigel. 'Wrote *The Lady of Shallots* and *The Charge of the Fire Brigade.'*

'And are your lordship's thoughts turning to love?'

'Oh yes, indeed they are, Mr Tombface. "Spring the sweet spring is the year's pleasant king." One must not waste one's youth.'

'A maxim I have always endeavoured to pass on to any young persons of my acquaintance. However, there is a slight problem with your lordship's aspirations.'

'A problem?'

'With respect, my lord…'

'Whenever you say that, Fiskers, I know immediately that you are about to become perfectly insolent.'

'I was only going to say that only through an act of the most abject sycophancy could your lordship be described as a young man. The world has had cause to be grateful for your existence for nearly eighty-three years.'

'Pah! Pish, piddle and butterscotch. You are talking out of your scrawny bottom. Eighty is not old! Eighty is the late flush of youth! Eighty is the new twenty-five! And besides, this is my *anus mirabilis*. Anything is possible. The Germoloids ointment has shrunk my piles. I have not had a gout attack for weeks. Fiskerton, I am going to STAND UP! I AM WALKING TO THE SIDEBOARD. I am pouring a glass of Sercial. I am walking back to my wheelchair. I shall walk a little further each day. This summer, Fiskerton, we shall play the local peasants at cricket. The age of miracles is upon us.'

'I can only applaud your lordship's courage.'

'Quite. Now we must turn our attention to the fair sex.'

'Did your lordship have a particular damsel in mind?'

'Not a damsel, exactly, more of a matron. There was a clue in my little ditty just now.'

'You will have to enlighten me. I cannot decipher it.'

'Why, I mean Hippolyta, of course.'

'Ah.'

'Oh yes. Hippolyta, Dowager Countess Skellingthorpe of Hartsholme House. She. The only she.'

'Do you really plan to make her your mistress?'

'Mistress? What kind of filthy talk is that? Mistress? I plan to marry her. I am going to make her my wife.

'Lady Skellingthorpe? But you fight all the time. The last time you met, you nearly killed Dido, her lapdog. All is sweetness and light until you both get drunk and then it becomes a screaming match.'

'Mere banter, lad. You'd understand if you weren't such a terminal misery-knickers. The woman has no husband and no heir. She is minted; she is flush; she is rolling in it; she is obscenely filthy stinking rich. What is more, I am convinced that she is uncontrollably in love with me. Get thee to Hartsholme House, *instanter*, sweet cully, and invite her to dinner on Tuesday week. I shall propose to her, and we shall be married in Lincoln Cathedral in June.'

'That cannot be, your lordship.'

'"That cannot be?" You are impertinent, sir. Look to your place, sir, or I shall have you bullwhipped and thrown naked into the North Delph at Short Ferry. What d'ye mean by it, sir?'

'It cannot be - because your lordship is already married.'

'Twaddle!'

'I fear it is not twaddle, my lord. The marriage certificate is in the safe in the library. Your lordship was married in 1959 at Saint Fiasco's in the village, the bride's family having disowned her. Canon Scothern officiated as you were united in Holy Matrimony to the Hon. Dorothy Wragby of Wragby House. Your Best Man, Darius "Dimples" Doddington, a friend from the university, did not survive the stag night and I was obliged to step in. The bridesmaids were Dame Fifi Threekingham and the Hon. Susan Swaton-Spanby of Sutton Manor.'

'By gad, it's coming back to me. She was a bolter, wasn't she, Dorothy?'

'I'm afraid she was. Lady Lindum ran off with a croupier at Monte Carlo on the third day of the honeymoon. They fled to Hungary.'

'Hungary had triangular stamps, you know, with primroses. I had a beauty in my stamp collection as a boy. I say, wasn't there a girl involved as well? I remember now. Magyar Posta, she was called. Lovely bit of fluff. Should have married *her*.'

'I think your lordship may be a little confused. 'Magyar Posta' is what it said on the stamp. It means Hungarian Post Office.'

'It was a quite beautiful collection. I wonder where it is now.'

'In the attic with your toys: your rocking horse, your teddy, your first twelve-bore - and Nanny.'

'Did she ever come back - Lady Lindum, I mean, not Magyar Posta?'

'She wrote to you asking for a divorce, saying that she was prepared to admit to adultery and that her Hungarian lover was happy to be cited as correspondent. You refused. You said that you would never allow her to marry her croupier, and besides, she had left you to bring up your son without a thought for his welfare.'

'I have a son?'

'Indeed you do, your lordship. He was born the day before your wedding.'

'By God, yes! What happened to him?'

'When you returned to England with the child after Lady Lindum's flight, you had him christened at Saint Fiasco's. He became The Hon. Rupert Atahualpa De'Ath. Ten minutes later, you disinherited him.'

'Why was that?'

'You said you didn't like his face, and that he looked like a constipated chimpanzee.'

'I expect I had him exposed on a hillside. To be eaten by wolves.'

'The last wolf in England perished in the reign of Henry VII, my lord.'

'Did I have him raised by a poor shepherd and his faithful wife?'

'No.'

'Fairies?'

'None hereabouts. The answer is more prosaic. He was raised by Scampton's wife.'

'In the gatehouse?'

'In the gatehouse.'

'You mean my child was being raised on my estate without my knowledge?'

'Not exactly. You paid for his upbringing and his schooling at Uppingham and consequently at the London School of Economics but forbade his coming anywhere near the big house. You said the Bolter's Child was never to be named in your presence again.'

'I expect that's why I forgot about the whole business.'

'I expect so, your lordship.'

'Nevertheless, he must be found. This is my Year of Wonders. Find the boy, Fiskerton.'

'He will no longer be a boy. He will be in his sixties.'

'Do you bandy words with me, sir?'

'Certainly not, your lordship. It would be more than my life is worth.'

'You never spoke a truer word.'

Later

'Look here. Tucked away in a corner of *The Telegraph*. That walrus. Apparently, it has taken to basking on a slipway at Tenby. Apparently the tusky blighter had to be shooed away with a power hose to allow the lifeboat to be launched. It's an omen, I tell you.'

'No doubt, your lordship. But of what?'

'Either my Year of Marvels or the End Times, I imagine. *Telegraph* doesn't say.'

May 22nd

'Freedom Day! Run up the baronial banner! Let the church bells ring! Cry God for Harry, England, and St George!'

'Perhaps that invocation should be updated to include her present Majesty, your lordship?'

'Egad, you're right, Fiskers, Harbinger of Good Tidings. Cry God for *Lizzie*, England, and St George! Don't want to invoke the renegade ginger, do we?'

'Before your lordship becomes too excited, I think I should point out that there are certain provisos to the announcement.'

'Which are?'

'Which are that the so-called Freedom Day is not today...'

'Chiz.'

'...but is projected for June 21st. However, we are warned that it might have to be limited because of the rapid spread of the Indian variant. It is a question of a race between the vaccine and the virus.'

'Where? Where's the race? Market Rasen? Southwell? Doncaster? York?'

'I believe the race in question is a metaphor, your lordship.'

'Metaphor? Bally good name for a horse that. Metaphor. I like it. Put £50 on the nose for me next time it runs.'

June

June 1st

'No deaths from Covid-19 to report at all from yesterday, your lordship.'

'Alleluia!'

'First time since 2020.'

'O praise ye the Lord! All ye that hath breath.'

'There is good news for the economy too.'

'Speak!'

'Kraft-Heinz have said that they will invest £140 million in a factory that will make tomato ketchup in England for the first time since 1999.'

'Well, bully for the old economy and yoicks talley-ho and all that but tomato sauce is fearfully plebby stuff. I understand the proles put it on chips and everything else.'

'I am happy to confirm that the only chips served in this household are game chips.'

'Quite so.'

'However, there is a bottle of Heinz Tomato Ketchup in the pantry, your lordship.'

'Throw it out immediately.'

'I think your lordship will countermand that instruction when I remind him what purpose it serves.'

'Go on. I am agog.'

'Fish finger sandwiches.'

'Fish finger sandwiches.'

'With white bread.'

'With white bread.'

'Thickly buttered.'

'Thickly buttered.'

'With lashings of tomato ketchup.'

'With lashings of tomato ketchup. Make one immediately. No. Come back. Make three. What are you dithering for, you snail? Go!'

June 12th

'So the "Indian Varian" is to be called the "Delta Variant" to spare subcontinental sensibilities. What a lot of Tommyrot! They didn't spare the feelings of the people of Wolverhampton when they came up with the "Kent Variant", did they?'

'They did not, your lordship, possibly because Wolverhampton isn't in Kent.'

'Isn't it? I could have sworn it was. Doesn't matter. The principle still stands. They won't consider *my* feelings if a new variant is discovered in Lincolnshire. Oh no. My sensibilities can fly up the chimney when they discover the "Mablethorpe Variant" for all they care. You mark my words.'

'I imagine that they will simply ascribe the next letter in the Greek alphabet to the new mutation.'

'By golly, I can do that, Fiskers. We did Greek at school. My Latin may be a little rusty but I can remember my Greek. The alphabet at least. It's all I could be bothered to learn. It goes something like this:

Alpha Beta Gamma Delta...erm...*Ether Urethra*...hang on - I'll get it in a minute... *Foxtrot Kilo Lima Oscar*...erm... *Pie*, of course... *Sigmund Tango Cairo Vulva*...no!...*Volvo* and finally *Omega*

There you are. The next variant will be called the "Ether Variant"!'

'I am speechless before your lordship's scholarship.'

June 13th

'I shall go into dinner now, thank you, Fiskerton. Isn't the birdsong divine?'

'Avian vespers, indeed my lord.'

'Eh?'

'A veritable carillon of birdliness, might I venture to say?'

'Sometimes, Fiskerton, you talk the most absurd tosh.'

Later

'Thank you, Fiskerton. Excellent dinner. Top hole! Now would you leave the whiskey and cigars on the table by the pear tree at the orchard gate.'

'Certainly, sir, but may I remind you that you gave up smoking three years ago?'

'Did I? Egad. *Tempus Fugit*, old runner bean! What!'

'Indeed, sir. Would you require anything more, sir?'

'No, no, that will be all. See that Lady Skellingthorpe has all she needs, there's a good fellow, won't you? Those thick towels from Alexandria would make a rather spiffing present. Send them over to her woman with my compliments, and see that my linen suit and summer tie are laid out for the morning. I intend to make an impression for her visit tomorrow.'

'Your lordship could hardly fail to do that.'

'Do I detect a note of sarcasm in your tone. Fiskerton?'

'Oh no, sir. Must be a distortion in my diction caused by a slippage of the dentures.'

June 14th
The Servants' Hall
Lindum Towers

'I understand that Lady Skellingthorpe's visit was not a success, Mr Fiskerton.'

'I fear not, Mrs Washingborough. It might more properly be called a calamity.'

'Do tell.'

'After luncheon, which her ladyship was pleased to praise, particularly my sole *meunière* and your blueberry pavlova, his lordship proposed a stroll in the gardens. Now that he can walk with the aid of a stick, they proceeded in a slow but stately manner, with myself in attendance several paces behind, propelling the wheelchair in case his lordship might become fatigued, and Potterhanworth, her ladyship's woman, in attendance, should she have need of her.'

'All was well until they reached the arbour. Her ladyship asked for her parasol, and Potterhanwith obliged and withdrew. The dowager countess sat upon a bench beside the pleached hornbeam while I helped his lordship perform a manoeuvre which we had rehearsed several times, but which I had insisted, with equal frequency, was foolhardy.'

'And what was that manoeuvre, Mr Fiskerton?'

'I helped his lordship to his knees.'

'Good lord!'

'Indeed. He waved me away, and then, in very flowery language, he proposed marriage to her ladyship.'

'Lord save us. And did she accept?'

'She did not accept. She smiled; the smile became a grin; the grin became a giggle; the giggle became a laugh, and the laugh became hysterical.

'"Potterhanworth! Potterhanworth!" she cried, "come to my aid at once or I fear I shall flood m'knickers. Get up, you old fool!"

'But of course he couldn't. I was obliged to help him to his feet and into the wheelchair. Meanwhile, her ladyship returned to the house along with her woman, both of them now shrieking with laughter.

'However, his lordship had his revenge for the humiliation.'

'How so, Mr Fiskerton?'

'He fed Dido, her ladyship's repulsive pug, with a whole bar of laxative chocolate as the party was preparing to depart. He had bribed Scopwick to obtain the substance from the pharmacy in Lindum Village.'

'Despite the stench.'

'Despite the stench. The bribe was also intended to buy the boy's silence on the matter, and indeed, he vowed to utter never a word. However, a further bribe from me easily undid his promise. We know that the noxious little canine breaks odorous wind. I fear that her ladyship will have more than farts to deal with on her return to Hartsholme House.'

June 19th
Freedom Day

'Well, I must say this is a pretty bloody turn up for the books, Fiskerton. It appears that "Freedom Day" is to be postponed for another month. Is this true, faithful retainer?

'Alas, I fear it is.'

'O woe! Take down the flag. Strike the bunting. Tell Washingborough to feed the jellies and blancmanges to the pigs. There will be no champagne today.'

'I think that is most appropriate, your lordship. I think a period of abstention would be a fitting indication to the household of your disappointment at the Government's decision.'

'Abstention? Who said anything about abstention? Are you barking mad, Fiskerton? Bring me a bottle of Yellow Chartreuse immediately. No - two. I intend to sleep out this tedious interval.'

July

July 3rd

'I thought your lordship would like to know that Mr Hancock has resigned.'

'Who? Who the devil are you talking about? You wake me from my reverie to talk to me about a complete stranger? Oh, you mean Tony Hancock. How in blistering Hell can he resign? He's dead.'

'No, not Tony Hancock. The Health Secretary, Matt Hancock.'

'Why didn't you say so?'

'He was caught in a clinch with a colleague in a corridor in the Commons.'

'Spicy old dog! Didn't know he had it in him. Bit of snogging eh? Who caught him?'

'CCTV cameras.'

'The silly arse. Whole Palace of Westminster is stuck full of them. "O the night has a thousand eyes…" Prat Hancock - Brat Hancock - Rat Hancock - Twat Hancock - Matt Handjob - Matt Wan…'

'Come along, your lordship. It's time for your medication.'

July 11th

'Fiskerton, have you taken leave of your senses?'

'IT'S COMING HOME!'

'What is?'

'The cup!'

'Where's it been? Don't we have enough crockery?'

'IT'S COMING HOME!'

'Stop blowing that damned whistle, you cretinous simpleton! What on earth are you wearing?'

'I am wearing my England strip.'

'Don't you dare strip. That clobber is bad enough without you taking it off. Whatever possessed you? What are you thinking of wearing shorts when you have knees like that?'

'I am simply showing solidarity with my country's football team in tonight's cup match.'

'I have no interest whatsoever in so-called football. It is a plebby game for the proles. Now what is this cup you're jibber-jabbering about?'

'IT'S COMING HOME! The European Cup, of course.'

'We have no need of foreign crockery. If the EU have only one cup between them all, they can keep it. We don't need it.'

'Your lordship doesn't wholly understand. It is the final. Against Italy. We have been victorious against many other European countries and have reached the final.'

'Did we beat France?'

'No, but Switzerland did.'

'Hurrah! Did we beat Germany?'

'Yes, we did!'

'Italy, you say.'

'Yes!'

'Hmmm.'

'Would you care to watch it with me this evening, your lordship?'

'I would not.'

'Even if I provided some toothsome snacks.'

'I'd rather swim with sharks that had had no breakfast.'

'Really? I can't persuade you?'

'NO!! But I'll have the snacks anyway.'

Later

'I see from *The Daily Smellygraph* that Boris has said that wearing masks will no longer be mandatory and that we should use our common sense.'

'Indeed, your lordship. One could argue that it is another small step towards our regaining our ancient liberties.'

'I agree, Fiskerton, and yet the Leftwaffe are demanding more clarity. They always want more clarity. Is it because they are hard of study? Is it because they are constitutionally obtuse? If the Government were to announce that water is wet, that His Holiness the Pope is a catholic and that bears use the woods as a latrine, they would still demand more clarity.'

'Well, I think one could argue that 'common sense' is not necessarily a well-defined commodity.'

'Oh phooey. It is all perfectly clear to *me* although nobody could argue that I was, in any way, especially well-endowed with common sense.'

'With that I would have to concur, your lordship.'

That evening

'I really do think it is unnecessary for us to be wearing masks to watch the football, your lordship.'

'I am using my common sense.'

'But there are only two of us in the drawing room.

'Better safe than sorry. There are tens of thousands in that crowd. I am taking no chances.'

'But Covid-19 cannot be transmitted through a television screen.'

'You cannot know that. Now will you shut up. You have persuaded me to watch this and I can't have you blathering all the way through it.'

'I am abjectly sorry your lordship.'

'Yes, well then. Here come the teams. IT'S COMING HOME! FISKERTON, IT'S COMING HOME!'

Half-time

'It's in the bag, wouldn't you say, Fiskers?'
'I would be more cautious, I think, your lordship.'
'Brilliant start. I say, this is a very exciting game, old boot. Why didn't you tell me?'
'Very remiss of me, your lordship.'
'Now, let's take a look at these snacks. What is this?'
'It's a meat pie, my lord. Traditional.'
'This thing with anchovies and olives looks pretty. I'll have a slab of that. And pour me another beer.'
'Certainly.'
'Yum! What is this thing I'm eating?'
'*Pissaladière.*'
'Oh, I wouldn't say that. It's rather good.'

After the match
Fiskerton's Pantry

'Whatever was that atrocious bang, Mr Fiskerton? It did so make me jump. I dropped the fish kettle on my toe. and had a litter of kittens.'
'His lordship shot the television.'
'Oh, not again.'

'Third time this month, Mrs Washingborough. He was enraged by the penalty shoot out and threatened to dismiss me for persuading him to watch the game. I explained to him that shooting the television is extremely dangerous and a frightful fire risk, but he then threatened to shoot *me*. Then he sped off down the Long Gallery in his wheelchair taking pot shots at vases.'

'O heavens, he's not on the loose again, is he?'

'No, he is in bed, weeping like a child. I tried to take his service revolver from him, but he has hidden it again. He is lying there threatening a terrible revenge on the England squad, the referee and on Italy, by vowing never to eat pasta again.'

August

August 14th

'What are these culture wars, O shambling mentor? It's very confusing. As far as I can understand it, a black man was killed by a policeman in the United States, so they threw a statue into the sea at Bristol, and it's all because of "white privilege"?'

'It's rather more complicated than that your lordship.'

'Do you feel privileged, Fiskerton?'

'I feel privileged to work for your lordship.'

'Well, there you are then.'

'Then there is the question of gender.'

'I remember that from Latin: masculine, feminine and neuter - men, women and eunuchs.'

'Quite so. Except that there are those in the universities who claim that sex is non-binary, and that there are more than a hundred genders.'

'And do you agree with them, Fiskers?'

'I am disinclined to, your lordship.'

'Quite right. There are chaps and lady chaps and that's all there is to it. Oh, and whoopsies, of course, but they're still chaps. Known a few "friends of Dorothy" in my time.

Carlton Scroop was one. Wanted to be called "Primrose". Great beefy chap with a high voice. Had us in stitches at the club. You kept your back to the wall though.

'No, it's quite simple. Men have a Matt Hancock and women have a foof! End of story.'

'Quite so.'

'And norks.'

August 28th

'Shortage of lorry drivers, bare supermarket shelves, Nando's running out of chicken, McDonald's running out of milkshakes, no sausages for Northern Ireland, no toys for Christmas, no pigs-in-blankets for Christmas, no turkeys for Christmas, no Christmas, fish wearing pullovers. We're all going to hell in a Matt Handcart, Fiskerton. It is the END TIMES!'

'Calm yourself, your lordship, or you will have one of your funny turns. I am sure that these scenarios are much exaggerated. The gentlemen of the press like to give things a doomsday cast. But, I am puzzled, I must confess. What does your lordship mean by "fish in pullovers"?'

'I meant jerseys. It's here in the paper.'

'Oh, I see. You are under a slight misapprehension, I think. Perhaps your lordship skim-read the passage. France is at loggerheads with Jersey because it claims the island is not granting enough licences to French vessels to fish in British territorial waters. They say the issue must be resolved by November 1st.'

'Gunboats. Send in the gunboats!'

'A little premature? Maybe we should try diplomacy first?'

'Harrumph. Maybe. But, look here, Fiskerton. What on God's earth is a Nando?'

'I believe Nando's is a chain restaurant, of Afro-Portuguese origin. It is much beloved of young people because it specialises in spicy chicken. The nation's youth likes things hot.'

'Groo! Sounds nasty. Now you needn't tell me what a McDonald's is. I know. I wouldn't feed one to a dog (unless it were Dido, of course), but you could not persuade me to try one of their milkshakes. I would rather have a colonoscopy without anaesthesia.'

'I cannot say that the prospect appeals to me either, your lordship.'

'What? The colonoscopy or the milkshake? I wish you'd be more exact, Fiskerton.'

'Neither.'

'Now, I must say I am devilishly concerned about one aspect of this doom-mongering.'

'And that is?'

'Christmas, I couldn't bear it if Christmas were cancelled again.'

'I know, your lordship, I know.'

'I'm not so worried about the toys, you know. I could play with last year's toys.'

'That's a very mature attitude, your lordship.'

'Thank you. But I couldn't bear it if there were no pigs-in-blankets. I couldn't bear it.'

'There, there, your lordship. Old Fiskers is here. There *will* be pigs-in-blankets. I swear it!'

'Oh, Fiskers, what would I do without you?'

'I aim to please.'

'On second thoughts, I dare say I'd manage. But how can you be so sure that there will be pigs-in-blankets?'

'Because they are already in the freezer, my lord.'

August 30th

'Now, Fiskerton, after breakfast, I shall offer a nuptial proposal to Lady Skellingthorpe again. A think a brace of kippers would give me fortitude for the task.'

'Very well, your lordship.'

'Only this time, I shall do it by telephone. That way I shall not have to adopt a genuflectory attitude with the agonising consequences of such a posture. I shall make the call from my study. I am not to be disturbed, d'you hear? - Or eavesdropped upon either.'

'It would not cross my mind to engage in such a degenerate practice, my lord.'

'I should hope not.'

Later

'It is good to see your worship beaming from ear to ear. Am I to assume that your suit was a success?'

'You are not to assume anything of the kind. Her ladyship turned me down flatly.'

'In that case, I am at a loss to understand your lordship's buoyancy.'

'Ah, but there was no laughter this time, just exasperation. Don't you see, plunger head, that that is a sign of progress.'

'Really?'

'Really. I suppose I cannot expect that you, a total innocent in affairs of the heart, should know that a lady is permitted, nay obliged, to reject a gentleman three times before she accepts a proposal of marriage. I have not the faintest doubt that the dowager countess will accept my final proposal. Meanwhile, I'll let the bint stew for a bit.'

September

September 4th

'I say, Fiskerton, what is that frightful pong?'

'I fear, my lord, that as a result of the heatwave, the drains have become a trifle whiffy.

'Whiffy? Whiffy? It is worse than the aroma from the muck-spreading at Kirby Muxloe last week. It is worse than getting downwind of Scopwick on a hot afternoon. I dare say the Black Hole of Calcutta was less rank. It is more rancid than the miasma that arises from Dido, Lady Skellingthorpe's farting dog. Do something.'

September 18th

'I say, these boffins are working jolly hard, are they not, Fiskerton? Booster jabs. Flu jabs. One in each arm. Death by a thousand pricks. Get me booked in for both pronto, Tonto.'

'I will indeed, Kemo Sabe, though your lordship will be invited by the NHS to attend six months and one week after the second vaccination.'

'When will that be?'

'By my calculation it should be in early November.'

'But I am protected till then?'

'It is my understanding that the efficacy of the vaccine may begin to wane a little over time. but your lordship should be safe so long as you are not foolhardy.'

'When have you ever known me to be foolhardy?'

'Never, your lordship.'

'Is that a sarcastic grin creeping over your sly mouth, Fiskerton?'

'I have a mild toothache, sir. Your lordship might have witnessed a grimace.'

'Well, keep it to yourself. You know, Fiskerton, I wish the boffins would invent a vaccine that would prevent one losing on the gee-gees. I'd have it like a shot. Ha! Like *a shot*! Geddit? Oh never mind.'

'Hilarious, your lordship.'

'I'd have it in my other arm. Hang on, I haven't got another arm to spare, have I? I'd have it in me bum, if necessary, and then *Hi-yo, Silver awaaaaay!* (I'd have to stand in the stirrups, obviously, if I'd just had a jab in me bum).'

September 23rd

'Turn it off, Fiskerton, turn it off.'

'Might I enquire why, your lordship?'

'I have had it with the BBC News. Everything is a bally catastrophe: fire, floods, earthquakes, famine, war, pestilence, the budget, NHS in crisis, Nicola Splurgeon braying on about Bawris Jawhnson, Covid cases, Covid hospitalisations, Covid deaths, ailing economy, inflation, Article 16. Even if there is a speck of good news, it will be glossed over, and we will be taken to 'our Human Misery Editor' who every day will find somebody who is prepared to weep to camera, wiping away the tears with the little finger of her right hand so that we can see her latest nail job.

'For instance, it might be a a tanning salon owner from Droitwich with eight kids whose dads have all absconded, and who has been burgled for the fourth time this week and diagnosed with cancer and has three days to live. The moronic journalist will then say: "How are you feeling?" How is she supposed to be bloody feeling, you obtuse nit?

'And everybody wants more money from the government. But it's not the government's money, is it? It's taxpayer's money. It's my money. It's your money. Well, mine anyway.

'Even the weather is catastrophic: 71°F is a heat wave - 31°F threatens a new ice age - and a spot of drizzle is a deluge. Turn it off! Turn it off!'

'Are you sure you want me to turn it off, your lordship? I could just turn over to ITV.'

'Jumping Jesus, no! That Peston geezer might pop up with his one-word-at-a-time delivery. Spare me that. I'd have to shoot the telly again and it's getting a bit expensive.'

'As your lordship wishes.'

'Bad for one anyway, too much telly. I think I shall undertake some improving reading instead. Bring me this week's *Beano*.'

October

October 21

'Have the Bentley ready at two o'clock sharp.'

'Where are we going, your lordship?'

'To Hartsholme House. Fiskerton. I am going to take Lady Skellingthorpe by surprise. It's make or break day, old partridge. I am going to make my third proposal and will not be gainsaid. I shall be gallant but forceful, chivalrous but insistent, courteous but bold. I shall make her see the error of her ways. She will not be able to resist me now that I am out of my wheelchair again. Pass me my stick.

'When we arrive, it will be your task to distract Hackthotn, her ladyship's man, with some subterfuge while I take the *art nouveau* lift to her ladyship's chamber.

'You may then wait in the car, to which I shall presently return, either victorious or upon my shield.'

'But who's going to be carrying the shield if I am in the car?'

'Clodpole! Try not to be so pedantic.'

Later. At Hartsholme House. His lordship returns to the car

'Rejoice, Fiskerton. Her ladyship has consented to make me the happiest man alive.'

'Oh, congratulations, your lordship! There will be such joy at Lindum Towers. Was she difficult to persuade?'

'Not in the least. I wager she was planning to accept in any case. Besides, I caught her at a disadvantage. Her lady ship was in the bath.'

'Heavens! Was she shocked?'

'Not as much as I was. Her norks have travelled in a distinct southerly direction. Almost down to her knees.'

'But surely she was distressed at your coming upon her in her nakedness.'

'I shall ignore the impropriety of what you have just said, Fiskerton. She was not in the least concerned because she knows I've seen it all before, though not in such an advanced state of dilapidation.'

'Then I am the one to be shocked.'

'Don't be a prude, Fiskerton. It doesn't suit you. Correction. It does suit you - but stop it anyway.

'Now you must arrange for the banns to be read, starting this coming Sunday.'

'Very well, your lordship. If your lordship will communicate your wishes to me on our return to Lindum Towers, I will speak to Canon Scothern at his earliest convenience.'

'It was a momentous occasion, Mrs Washingborough, I don't mind telling you. It must be many decades since his lordship attended divine service at St Fiasco's, and everyone from the villages of Lindum Magna, Lindum Parva, and Lindum Puerorum was there to goggle. They crowded around the lychgate as we came in and men and boys doffed their caps, and women and girls bobbed with bowed heads. A man at the back shouted: "God bless your lordship!" and another cried: "Long life to Baron Lindum!" And there was a ripple of applause. They are all his tenants, of course, and live in constant fear of eviction.

'We entered the building, and his lordship and I installed ourselves in his lordship's box pew, Scampton sitting in the pew behind. Scopwick, who had arrived on his filthy bicycle, was not allowed in the building.'

'Because of the stench.'

'Because it was assumed that even the Almighty would prefer His House not to be polluted by Scopwick's egregious aroma, and would be contented for the boy to perform a private act of worship in the churchyard.'

'Did the service go well, Mr Fiskerton?'

'Yes, and no, Mrs Washingborough. In itself, it was quite charming, but I am sorry to report that his lordship did not always display the composed piety one might have hoped for.'

'How so, Mr Fiskerton?'

'He sang the hymns lustily enough, if slightly off key, and he fidgeted through the psalms. During the bidding prayers, he terrified a choir boy by pretending to fix him in the cross hairs of an imaginary rifle, using his index fingers as the cross. He pretended to snore during the sermon and after five minutes shouted: "Wind it up, Scothern, you old drunk. You're boring everyone to death." During the Prayer for the Queen's Majesty, he stood to attention and then turned round to the congregation and bellowed: "On your feet, you miserable sinners, at the name of your Queen." There was quite a scramble because everyone was kneeling at the time.

'Then came the reading of the banns, at which his lord-ship began to rub his hands in glee.'

'There is one thing that is troubling me, Mr Fiskerton.'

'And what might that be, Mrs Washingborough?'

'How is it that the wedding is not to take place in Lady Skellingthorpe's parish church?'

'That is indeed the usual practice, but I'm afraid her ladyship blotted her copybook long ago. It is *une sale histoire*, as they say across the channel, a sordid tale. At her marriage to the Earl of Skellingthorpe in the distant past, the beha-viour of the bride and groom was so appalling that the rector of St. Pomfret's Hartsholme, the Rev. Horace Stickney, barred them from the congregation until a proper contrition and amendment of conduct might be manifest. Of course, that never happened. When the Earl died, some ten years later, the rector relented, and permitted the service for the burial of the dead to take place at his church, though his widow was kept under constant surveillance.'

'What had happened at their wedding was this: The noble groom and his best man, the Duke of Kesteven, arrived, already drunk, and they placed a number of bottles of champagne in the font to chill. Soon, the bride came down the aisle, also much the worse for wear from alcohol, with a black Sobranie cigarette in a holder protruding from under her veil.

'Halfway down the aisle she kicked off her bridal slippers, and danced a barefoot little jig all the way up to her husband to be. The congregation could all see that her bridal train had been caught up in her unmentionables, but her equally intoxicated bridesmaids' attempts to fix this came to nothing for she simply batted their fumbling hands away.

'After the ceremony, she gave the rector a lengthy kiss full on the lips, and danced a can-can in the chancel, emitting little screams the while. Wolf whistles were heard. Is it any wonder the rector was scandalised?'

'Mr Fiskerton, you have made me blush. But pray go on and tell me about the reading of the banns.'

'Very well. When it came to the time for parish notices, Canon Scothern pronounced the solemn words: "I publish

the banns of marriage between, Hippolyta Tabitha Cherry-
bloom Possett, of no fixed parish [a form of words I sugges-
ted, Mrs Washingborough] and Aubyn Xerxes Arbuthnot
De'ath, of this parish. If any of you know cause or just im-
pediment why these persons should not be joined together in
Holy Matrimony, ye are to declare it. This is the first time of
asking."

'Well, at this point, his lordship grabbed my knee and
squeezed it with such ferocity that I nearly passed out with
the pain.

'"Not a word," he hissed in my ear. Then he turned to
glare at the congregation over his shoulder. It was a look that
would have frozen over hell.'

'Why was his lordship so troubled by the banns, Mr
Fiskerton?'

'Ah, I remember the cause, Mrs Washingborough, but
you do not. It is perhaps best left just so. I hope morning service at St Periwig-the-Less at Lindum Cloaca was less event-
ful?'

'It was not too well-attended, Mr Fiskerton, but the vicar
was pleased to receive a jar of my lemon curd.'

October 25th

'Holy socks! It says here that police have shot dead a
rare white deer that was wandering the streets of Bootle. By
the Lord Harry, if my hunting days were not over, there'd

have been no need for the police. Where is Bootle? Is it near Scunthorpe?'

'No, your lordship, it is near Liverpool, quite the other side of the country.'

'Pity. If it had been nearer, I might have got back on horseback to hunt down any friends this white deer might have, wandering the streets, terrorising the poor people of Bootle. White deer would have been even rarer in Bootle then, believe you me.'

'A likely story.'

What?'

'I said, "You'd have covered yourself in glory."'

'Pretty stupid animals though. Don't you think so, Fiskerton? I mean white is a pretty stupid colour if you want to camouflage yourself. Especially in Bootle.'

October 28th

'I hear on the wireless that there are severe petrol shortages at garages in England, your lordship.'

'Is this the BBC again, mongering doom? There's possibly one garage in some suburb of London that no-one's ever heard of, that's had a late delivery, and that's all.'

'Possibly, your lordship.'

'But if it is true, we cannot have a fuel shortage jeopardise my wedding. Fill up the cars. Scour every garage in the land. Leave no pump undrained. Fill every container you can find. Cans, bottles, pans, bedpans. Make sure her ladyship's Daimler is full to the gunwales. Steal fuel if necessary. Siphon it off in the dead of night.'

'The suggestion is that the shortage will be short-lived, your lordship, and, in any case, your lordship should steel himself to the idea that the wedding will not be taking place in the near future if the divorce is not completed in time.'

'Hush, no-one must know of the divorce. There will be plenty of time. The banns must be read twice more. Why are these lawyers so *slow*?'

'Because delay equals income, your lordship?'

'Go into Lincoln tomorrow and harry my solicitors, Tetford, Belchford and Baumber. They must press to have the business completed.'

October 29th

'Well, what news, Fiskerton? Spout, man! Don't stand there gasping like a landed fish. Speak!'

'Mr Belchford sends his compliments to your lordship, and begs to submit his apologies. It appears that the delay is very much down to your first wife's notary in Hungary. However, Mr Belchford will do what he can to expedite the matter.'

'Damned mealy-mouthed scoundrel! Ha! You'll wait till Doomsday for your fee, Mr Fartnasty Belchford, if you don't pull your finger out of your fundament.'

'Mr Baumber did have some positive news, however. Your son has been located.'

'What? How? Where?'

'It transpires that he read law at university, did well, moved to the United States, became lawyer to the stars, made a fortune, and has a mansion on Pacific Heights in San Francisco. He is worth millions.'

'How marvellous! Truly this is a year of wonders! Get Baumber to contact him, and tell the boy to come home. Ask him if he can lend me a few grand. Tell him all is forgiven.'

'I am afraid that will not work, your lordship. The Hon. Mr De'Ath, as he styles himself, wants nothing to do with you.'

'How sharper than a serpent's tooth it is to have a thankless child!'

'It was you who disinherited him when he was less than a fortnight old.'

'Yes, but I didn't know he would turn out to be stinking rich, did I? Send him a wedding invitation. That should melt his stony heart.'

November

november 1st

'I fear your union cannot be solemnised until the decree absolute is obtained.'

'Sodomised?'

'Certainly not, your lordship. Solemnised. Your marriage cannot be celebrated until the divorce is complete.'

'Oh that doesn't matter. Nobody will mind. This is Lincolnshire, man. They go in for inbreeding in these parts. In Sleaford, many people have six fingers. In Boston, they wave webbed feet. In Skegness, two heads. A little matter of temporary bigamy is of no account. And Canon Scothern will be placated with a few tins of Special Brew and a packet of Marlboro.'

November 2nd
His Lordship and Fiskerton are listening to the news on the wireless.

'Greta Thunberg, aged 18, stood in Govan Festival Park leading a chorus of "You can shove your climate crisis up your arse."'

'Disgraceful! If that demented child continues to aspire to sainthood, Fiskerton, she needs to watch her buggering language!'

November 3rd

'What is this Insulate Britain business, Fiskerton? Why should people protest about some chaps coming round to insulate their lofts? Eh? Don't make sense.'

'That is not quite their case, your lordship, they are protesting that not enough people are insulating their houses fast enough to make any significant difference to the rate of climate change, and that the government is not doing enough to help.'

'Well, there's not a lot I can do about Lindum Towers, is there? Too big and draughty. Would cost the earth. And the East Wing has fallen down. No point in insulating that. Besides, do they not know the price of coal these days? I can't afford to heat the house and insulate it as well. So what form is this protest taking? Loonies marching up and down in fancy dress?

'No, your lordship. It is more radical than that. They have been blocking slip roads on to the M25 and other motorways by sitting in the road. When they are removed, someone else takes their place. Some have even glued themselves to the road.'

'What? They put Pritt on their bottoms?'

'No, your lordship.'

'Cow gum? Fish glue?'

'No, your lordship. Superglue. They glue their hands and other parts of the body to the road. I believe one person even glued his face to the road.'

'Hot crumpets! Are they deranged?'

'They are not popular. Their actions are highly disruptive. One woman even glued her exposed breasts to the tarmac.'

'SHE GLUED HER NORKS TO THE PAVEMENT?'

'Just the one, as I understand it, your lordship.'

November 6th

'Look, look at what Boris has said at the Climate Summit: "It is one minute to midnight on that Doomsday clock and we need to act now." I told you. It is the END TIMES! Up on the roof! The waters are rising!'

'I think there is no need for immediate panic, your lordship. I fancy the Prime Minister was speaking metaphorically. Besides, here is a letter from Mr Belchford containing excellent news.'

'How do you know?'

'I steamed it open, your lordship.'

'Why?'

'In the interests of security.'

'Very well. What does it say?'

'It says that the decree absolute has been granted. The divorce is complete. Your lordship is free to marry! The relevant documents will be sent by courier later this morning.'

'Oh, rapture! Get in touch with Canon Scothern and fix the day. We shall be married on Advent Sunday!'

'Very well, I shall do so. I have also received a communication from your son, via Mr Baumber. He says he will not be attending the wedding but sends a cheque for $5 for a buttonhole.'

'The cheeky blighter! I like his impudence. Chip off the old block, what!'

November 25th
The Paddock where a marquee is being erected for the reception

'I believe I have never seen his lordship so chipper, Mr Fiskerton.'

'Indeed, Mr Scampton, he is quite a new man. And what is most remarkable is that the old skinflint is spending as if there will be no tomorrow. One suspects that the money he is spending is Lady Skellingthorpe's, but no matter, his bounty knows no bounds.'

'This marquee must be costing a pretty penny, along with the beer tent for the villagers, the Punch and Judy and other entertainments for the children.'

'Not to mention preparations for the feast, Mr Scampton. As Mrs Washingborough refused to come up to receive his instructions, his lordship came down to her in the kit-chens. You know she has refused to see him face to face for many years. Well, when she had finished screaming and wav-ing the fire tongs about, his lordship bid her sit down and told her that she need not worry her head about the fare for the reception. He intended to hire caterers, but he would be obliged nevertheless if she would make many jellies in all the colours of the rainbow and cocktail sausages on sticks stuck in potatoes to look like hedgehogs.

'He then said he was doubling her salary. As you can imagine, she broke down in tears. "What a lovely man he is, to be sure," she said, "I have took him wrong all these years."'

'And I understand, Mr Fiskerton, that his lordship was so amused at his son's buttonhole cheque that he has rescinded the disinheritance and restored Mr De'Ath in his will. Even-tually, he will become the fifth Baron Lindum.'

'I believe Mr De'Ath also had something to communicate to your good self.'

'He has invited Mrs Scampton and myself to visit him at his mansion in California, all expenses paid, to thank us for raising him. I fear we cannot accept until he and his lordship are reconciled, which I hope to bring about 'ere long.'

'Look, Mr Scampton, there is his lordship, talking to the men and waving his arms about. He has become quite sprightly of late.'

'I am afraid he is getting in the way of their work rather frequently. I passed by yesterday as he was haranguing the foreman, and overheard him say: "And do you know, she glued her norks to the pavement."'

Epilogue
Advent Sunday

And so Aubyn Xerxes Arbuthnot Evelyn De'Ath, Fourth Baron Lindum of Lindum Towers in the County of Lincolnshire was married to his bride Hippolyta, Dowager Countess Skellingthorpe, of Hartsholme House, Canon Scothern officiating. The Best Man was Billy 'Bulldog' Bassingham, an Oxford friend of his lordship, and the Matron of Honour was Gertrude Grange-de-Lings.

The bride wore a low-cut dress of white tulle and a veil of white Breton lace. She carried a bouquet of Agapanthus lilies, signifying purity, all of which promoted some inappropriate mirth amongst the local peasantry. She also wore a red garter over white silk stockings which caused a sensation at the reception held later at Lindum Towers.

Young Jack Scopwick, having been put through a sheep dip, hosed down, bathed, given a hair cut and a manicure, and anointed with his lordship's most expensive toilet water, was the page boy, dressed in a pink satin suit of his own design.

On the same day, Archibald Fiskerton of Lindum Towers was married to Nora Washingborough, also of Lindum Towers, following a brief courtship.

And on the same day, Mr and Mrs Josiah Scampton renewed their wedding vows.

During the reception, Scopwick made a little speech, announcing that he was gay, after which he eloped to Brighton with the butcher's boy - to wild applause.

The multi-coloured jellies were consumed, and much champagne was quaffed. The speeches were scandalous, and the revels continued well into the following day.

And they all lived happily ever after.

Reviews for the prequel to this book

Lord Lindum's Anus Horribilis

Winner of the Chill with a Book Special PB Award

Rubbish

Reviewed in the United Kingdom on 5 February 2021
Verified Purchase
Absolute drivel. A complete waste of money and time. Very poorly
thought out and full of weak jokes.

Amazon Reader

Hilarious

Reviewed in the United Kingdom on 27 November 2020
Verified Purchase
Outrageous, hilarious and borderline surreal, Ian Thomson's mon-
strous creation and his long-suffering but devious butler Fiskerton
are unforgettable in this romp through the unique challenges of
2020. Richly entertaining - the perfect gift!
L. Bromley

Printed in Great Britain
by Amazon